W9-AUA-213

My "I" Sound Box®

WRITTEN BY JANE BELK MONCURE • ILLUSTRATED BY REBECCA THORNBURGH

Published by The Child's World®
1980 Lookout Drive • Mankato, MN 56003-1705
800-599-READ • www.childsworld.com

ISBN HARDCOVER: 9781503823150
ISBN PAPERBACK: 9781503831377
LCCN: 2017960361

Printed in the United States of America
PA02371

A NOTE TO PARENTS AND EDUCATORS:

Magic moon machines and five fat frogs are just a few of the fun things you can share with children by reading books with them. Reading aloud helps children in so many ways! It introduces them to new words, motivates them to develop their own reading skills, and expands their attention span and listening abilities. So it's important to find time each day to share a book or two . . . or three!

As you read with young children, you can help develop their understanding of how print works by talking about the parts of the book—the cover, the title, the illustrations, and the words that tell the story. As you read, use your finger to point to each word, modeling a gentle sweep from left to right.

Simple word games help develop important prereading skills, including an understanding of rhyme and alliteration (when words share the same beginning sound, such as "six" and "sand"). Try playing with words from a book you've just shared: "What other words start with the same sound as moon?" "Cat and hat, do those words rhyme?" The possibilities are endless—and so are the rewards!

My "I" Sound Box®

Little had a box. "I will find things that begin with my **I** sound," he said.

"I will put them into my sound box."

Little looked under some leaves and found lizards. Did he put the leaves and the lizards into his box? He did.

Then Little 🧒 looked behind some logs
and found lambs. They were little lambs.

"You must be lost," said Little . So he put the little lambs and the logs into the box with the leaves and the lizards.

Then Little walked to a lake.

The lizards leaped out of the box. But Little put

them back. "I do not like leaping lizards," he said.

Little looked in the lake and found a lobster.

He lifted the lobster into the box . . . carefully

. . . because the lobster had long claws.

Then Little saw a lighthouse by the lake.

He went inside the
lighthouse. The lantern
was not on. So Little
climbed up the
ladder . . .

. . . and lit the lantern.

"Someone might be

lost," he said.

Little heard a loud roar. He opened

the door and found a little lion.

The little lion licked him. The little lion sat in his lap.

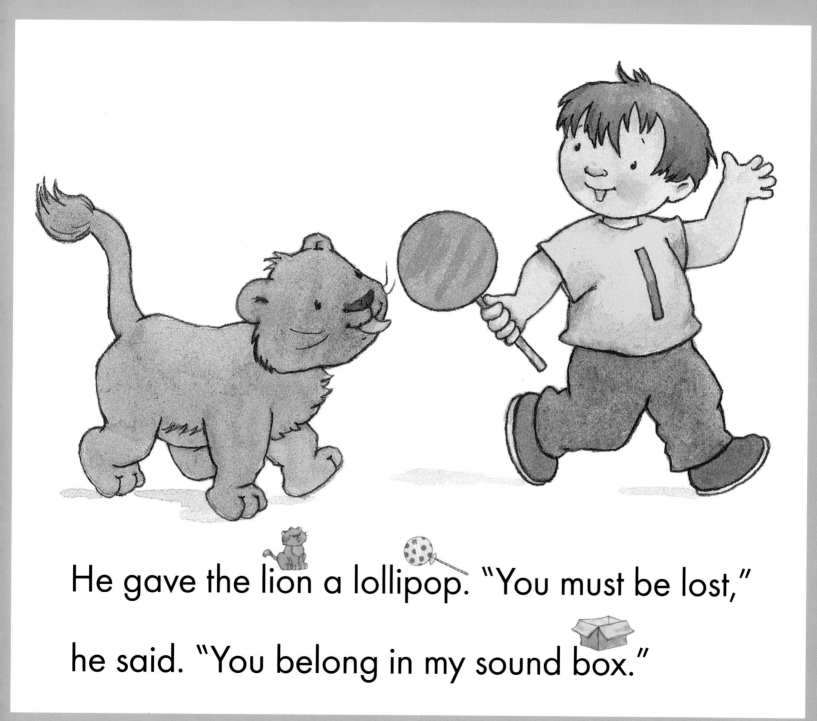

He gave the lion a lollipop. "You must be lost," he said. "You belong in my sound box."

Little heard another loud roar. He opened

the door and found a little leopard.

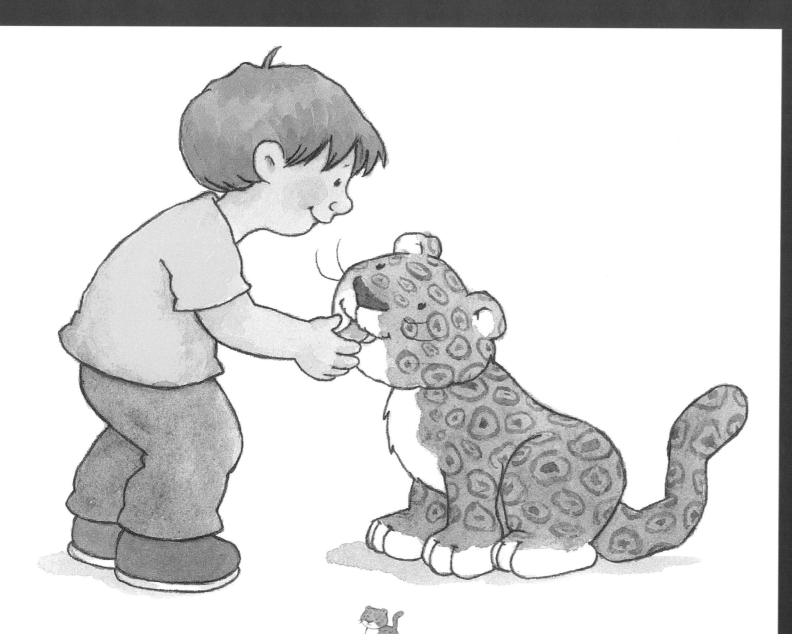

The little leopard licked him.

The little leopard sat in his lap.

Little gave the leopard a lollipop.

"You must be lost," he said. "You

belong in my sound box."

But when he put the little leopard into the box . . .

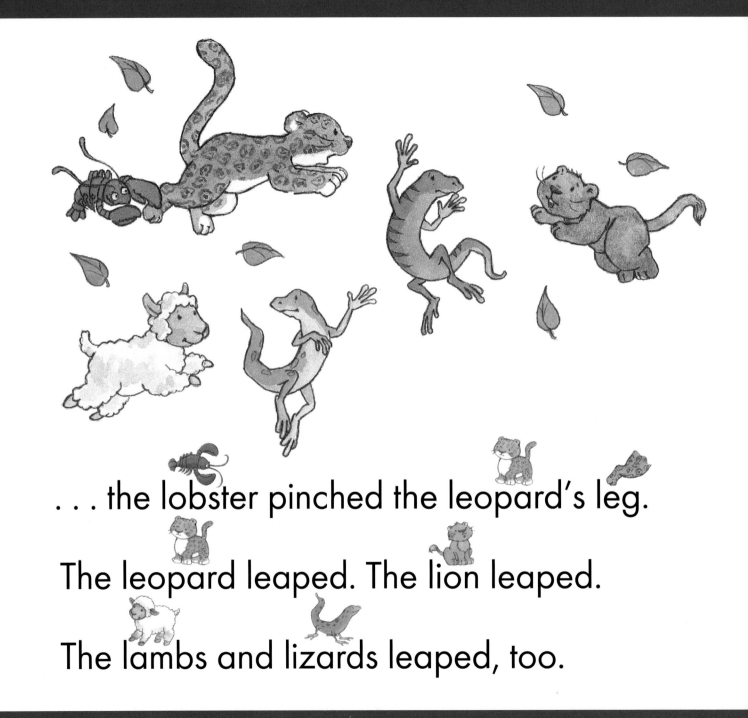

. . . the lobster pinched the leopard's leg.

The leopard leaped. The lion leaped.

The lambs and lizards leaped, too.

So Little put the lobster into a lobster pot.

Just then, he heard another loud roar. He

opened the door and saw a locomotive.

"Let's go for a long ride!" he said.

Little Word List

ladder

leaves

lizard

lake

leg

lobster

lamb

leopard

locomotive

lantern

lighthouse

log

lap

lion

lollipop

28

Other Words with Little

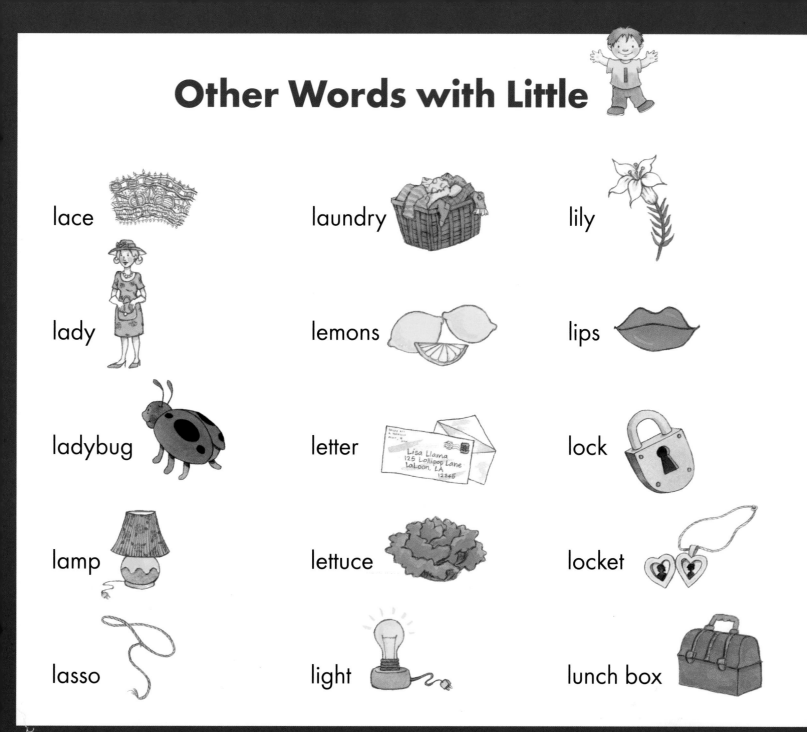

lace

lady

ladybug

lamp

lasso

laundry

lemons

letter

lettuce

light

lily

lips

lock

locket

lunch box

More to Do!

Little had a good time with all the animals!
He wrote to his friend, Lily, about his adventures.

Dear Lily,

Today I looked in some leaves and logs. I found lizards and lambs! The lizards kept leaping out of my box. I do not like leaping lizards.

Next I went to the lake and saw a lighthouse. Can you guess what I found when I went inside? I found a little lion and a leopard. I gave each of them a lollipop.

We all took a ride on a locomotive. It was a very fun day.

Love,

Little l

Lisa Llama
125 Lollipop Lane
LaLoon, LA
12345

Try It!

You can write to someone you love, too. Write about what you did today. You can tell the person that you read a book about the sound of l!

About the Author

Best-selling author Jane Belk Moncure (1926–2013) wrote more than 300 books throughout her teaching and writing career. After earning a master's degree in early childhood education from Columbia University, she became one of the pioneers in that field. In 1956, she helped form the Virginia Association for Early Childhood Education, which established the first statewide standards for teachers of young children.

Inspired by her work in the classroom, Mrs. Moncure's books became standards in primary education, and her name was recognized across the country. Her success was reflected not only in her books' popularity with parents, children, and educators, but also by numerous awards, including the 1984 C. S. Lewis Gold Medal Award.

About the Illustrator

Rebecca Thornburgh lives in a pleasantly spooky old house in Philadelphia. If she's not at her drawing table, she's reading—or singing with her band, called Reckless Amateurs. Rebecca has one husband, two daughters, and two silly dogs.